PUP, PUP AND AWAY!

PaRragon

Bath • New York • Cologne • Melbourne • Delhi
Hong Kong • Shenzhen • Singapore

It was the day of the Annual Mayor's
Balloon Race, and Adventure Bay's
own Mayor Goodway was nervous.
   "Why did I agree to a balloon race?"
she said, covering her eyes. "I have
to get over my fear of heights."

"Don't worry. I'll be in the balloon to help you," said Ryder. "Ready to check the balloon, pups?"

"Ready, Ryder, sir!" Rubble barked.

Rubble and Chase checked the dusty balloon.
"Uh-oh!" Chase said. "It's got a ... a ... *ACHOO!*"
When he had stopped sneezing from the dust,
he continued, "... a hole! A ripped balloon can't
hold air!"

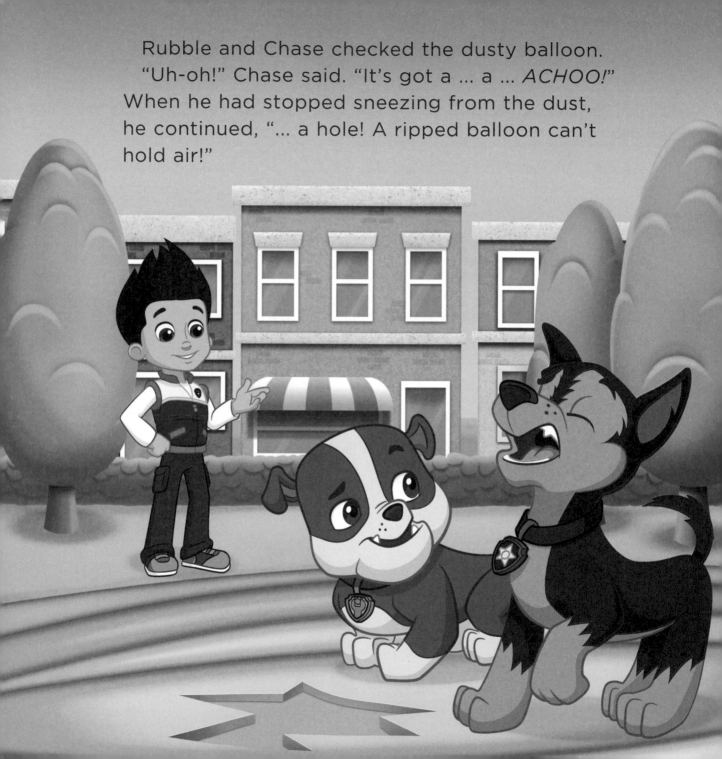

Mayor Goodway groaned. "That means Mayor Humdinger from Foggy Bottom will win again!"

"Don't worry," Ryder said. "We'll get this balloon ready for the race. No job is too big, no pup is too small."

So Ryder pulled out his PupPad and called the rest of the PAW Patrol.

The PAW Patrol quickly assembled at the Lookout.
"Ready for action, Ryder, sir!" Chase barked.
Ryder told the pups about the mayor's balloon.
"We need to fix the balloon for the race. Rocky, can
you find something in your recycling truck to patch it up?"

"Don't lose it, reuse it!" Rocky said.

"And the hot air that makes the balloon rise comes from a gas flame," Ryder continued. "Marshall, I'll need you to make sure the heater is safe."

"I'm all fired up!" Marshall replied.

The PAW Patrol raced to the town square. Rocky quickly inspected the tear in the balloon. "I've got the perfect patch in my truck," he said.

"And how do the gas tanks look?" Ryder asked.

"The big question is – how do they smell?" Marshall replied. He sniffed the tanks. "I don't smell any gas leaks."

Rocky glued a piece of Zuma's old surf kite over the hole.
"Good work!" Ryder said. "That patch is a perfect fit."
Ryder turned a lever and the balloon slowly filled with
hot air. The other balloons were gathering on the horizon.
The race was about to begin....

"It's time to get over my fear of heights,"
the mayor shouted. "I'm going to win this race!"
She pumped her fist and accidentally hit the lever
on the heater. The balloon started to fly away.

Marshall jumped up and grabbed the rope with his teeth. But the balloon didn't stop. Instead, Marshall was pulled high into the air. Suddenly, the rope slid from Marshall's mouth and he fell!

Luckily, Marshall landed in Ryder's arms.
"Thanks, Ryder!" he barked.

The race had started and there was no
time to waste. Ryder called Skye on his PupPad.
"Mayor Goodway took off without me. I need
you to fly me to her balloon in your helicopter."

Skye slid into her Pup House, which quickly
turned into a helicopter. "Let's take to the sky!"
she called out, zooming into the air.

Skye flew to Ryder and dropped a harness down to him.
He locked himself in and then Skye whisked him away.
"I'll swing you over to the balloon," Skye said.

Ryder sailed
through the air,
reached out and
caught hold of
the basket!

Mayor Goodway helped Ryder climb into the balloon. Then Ryder gave it a quick burst of hot air and it rose over the lighthouse.

"Made it, Skye," Ryder reported as he undid his harness.

"All right, Mayor Goodway, are you ready to win this race?"
The mayor gave Ryder a thumbs-up. "I'm in it to win it!"
Then Ryder and the mayor raced after the other balloons.

With Ryder at the controls, the balloon quickly
caught up with Mayor Humdinger, who was in the lead.
"The race is on!" Ryder yelled.
"I have never lost a race and I'm not going to now!"
Mayor Humdinger shouted back.

With a rush of hot air, Ryder and Mayor Goodway's
balloon whooshed past Mayor Humdinger's balloon.
  "There's Jake's Mountain!" Mayor Goodway exclaimed.
"The finish line is just on the other side!"

"The winds are stronger higher up,"
Ryder said. "We'll have a better chance
of winning if we go up and use them."
"Up, up and away!" cheered the mayor.

Ryder guided the balloon higher and they rode the rushing winds over Jake's Mountain. But Mayor Humdinger did the same! His balloon zipped right past Ryder and Mayor Goodway.

Down on the ground, the PAW Patrol pups cheered as the balloons came into view. Mayor Goodway and Ryder dropped in ahead of Mayor Humdinger at the last second and crossed the finish line first. They won the race!

Mayor Humdinger glumly handed the trophy to Mayor Goodway. "I believe this belongs to you."

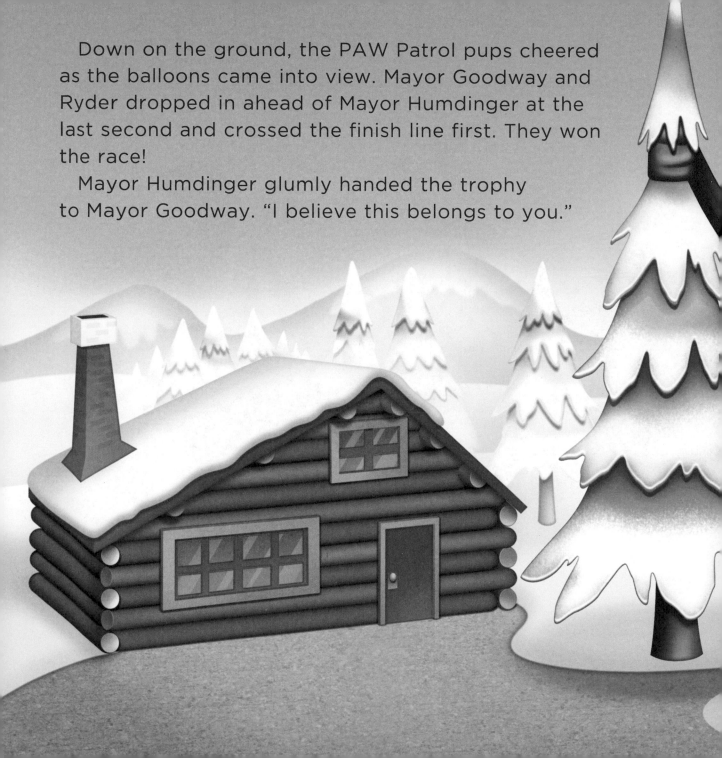

Mayor Goodway gave the trophy to Ryder.
"This really belongs to Ryder and the PAW Patrol."
Ryder smiled with pride. "Thanks, Mayor Goodway!"